I'm a Victim

of

Circumstances

Nataisha T. Hill

Published by TaiLorMade Books

Chapter 1

"Lisa, you did an excellent job on Mrs. Cornfield's make-up! And to reward you for your continual excellence, I will be buying you lunch on Friday."

"Oh, how nice. Thank you, Ms. Greene."

"You are so welcome! If you keep this up, you'll be lead of your department in no time."

"All you gotta do is add three more years to your existing four years," Helen mocked, after their supervisor left.

"It's not funny, Helen. I'm sick and tired of these damn five cent raises every year. I come to work on time, I do twice as many faces than anyone on the team, and I work late."

"Lisa, it's not hard to make a sixty-eight-year-old lady feel better about herself."

"You're such a hater," Lisa said, playfully tossing a lip liner sample at her. "I don't see you in high demand for makeup services."

"Well, we can't help it if the customer requests you. What do you want us to do, take their cane and force them to sit down?"

"Whatever, Helen. I'm not blaming anything on you guys. I'm just saying that if an employee is outperforming most of her colleagues, there should be some type of additional compensation."

"Well, she is paying for your lunch Friday, so technically-"

"Don't even go there," Lisa interrupted.

Lisa sighed as she sat in her makeup chair looking in the mirror. She was a beautiful twenty-six-year-old woman with a killer figure and no kids. When she first started working in the makeup department at Macy's, she thought she had found her dream job. She loved making women look beautiful. She even met her husband, Terry there.

However, Lisa longed to have the finer things in life. She wanted to be the one taking glam shots while thousands of followers loved per pictures. Perhaps she could even be a MUA for the stars. But, for now, she was stuck in a small town with a local mall that mainly served old ladies.

It was a little after six by the time Lisa had arrived home. She and Terry stayed in a nice-sized two bedroom duplex a few miles outside of town. It was newly remodeled with updated appliances and a huge master bathroom. The rent wasn't much since her husband's dad owned the unit.

"Terry, we got another late notice for our water bill in the mail. I thought you told me last week that you handled it," Lisa yelled, after sitting down at the kitchen island.

"I told you that I will handle it. I also explained to you several weeks ago that business has been slow, so my dad pays me bi-weekly now."

"Terry, this bill is due monthly. You just got paid three days ago."

"I forgot to pay the damn bill, okay? My brother needed to borrow money for diapers, so I gave it to him."

"Why didn't he just ask your parents for the money like he always does?"

"Because he didn't ask my parents, he asked me. We can't keep depending on mom and dad for every small issue."

"If your brother isn't able to afford something as simple as a diaper, that's a huge issue. Perhaps his wife needs to get up off her ass and get a job."

"Perhaps you need to mind your own damn business and worry about yourself like you always do. At least my brother's wife will give him kids. She isn't worried about messing up her perfect little figure like you are."

"Let's be clear, her figure was never perfect. Plus, I told you before we got married that kids weren't in the near future."

"Okay, and I gave you almost four years to do whatever it was you wanted to do."

"Who are you to put a time limit on my freedom?"

"I am your husband, Lisa. When people get married, that's what they do. They make sacrifices and raise a family."

"Babies cost money, Terry! If you can't afford to pay a damn water bill, how in the hell are you gonna pay the medical bills, formula, pampers, clothes, and all the baby items that come with having a baby. What are you gonna do, ask mommy and daddy for the money?"

"Okay, so now you want to talk to me like I'm less than a man. I'm out of here," he said, walking off. "You know what though," he added, turning back around, "perhaps you're right. Maybe we shouldn't have kids since my parents can't stand you. They'll probably end up not liking the kids either."

"I don't give a damn, Terry. If your parents choose not to be in our kid's life, then that's on them. I'm not going to beg them to do anything. All I've ever done was been nice to your parents. If they don't like me it's because of something that you're telling them."

"Your actions speak volumes, Lisa."

"Okay, so what have I done to personally fall out of your parents' grace?"

"Look, I'm done with this conversation. I'll pay the damn bill when I get some money," he said, slamming the door on his way out of the house.

Lisa knew that this would be yet another night where Terry would hang out with his friends and get drunk. She was extremely sick of his attitude the past few months and him pressuring her about kids. He had no right to rush her into something that was discussed before they agreed to get married. Lisa called her mom who told Lisa that she shouldn't throw in the towel just yet. Lisa didn't want to throw away three years of marriage, but Terry was seriously pushing her in that direction.

Chapter 2

It was Friday and Lisa went to work feeling optimistic. Terry had bought her roses and cooked her a candle-lit meal the night before in order to make up with her for being an asshole. What she enjoyed the most was the make-up sex. It was always over the top after they argued. On a regular basis the sex was only moderately satisfying. This was definitely not the case after an altercation. He'd give her oral sex until she had to push his head away from the intensity of the orgasm. It was actually a great way to start her day.

"Lisa, you'll never guess what I heard?"

"What is it this time, Helen?"

"Ms. Greene is throwing in the tile. Wouldn't it be great if you could take her place?"

"No, I don't want to stop doing makeup. I just want more compensation."

"Oh my gosh! A person like you can never be satisfied."

"That's not true. I was overly satisfied last night."

"Okay, no one wants to hear about your dull married life."

"Oh really?" Lisa said in a challenging tone, making sure no customers were in sight. "My dull married life is better than wild whorish escapades of screwing men in dressing rooms." She whispered.

"You bitch!" Helen whispered back with a mischievous grin.

A few hours had passed and the work day was still going great. Ms. Greene had actually bought her whole team Olive Garden opposed to only Lisa. Even though the food was delicious, it took away the point of Lisa getting rewarded. Perhaps someone went to Ms. Greene and expressed that everyone deserved a pat on the back. Her colleagues were always jealous and catty like that.

Shortly after lunch, Ms. Greene had walked over to their counter. She had a confused look on her face opposed to the giddy expression that she normally carried. Lisa then figured that Helen had heard right. Ms. Greene had come by to say that this was her final two weeks. Now, it made since why she decided to feed the entire team.

"Uh...Lisa? I'm afraid that I have some bad news. If you don't mind, I think its best that we spoke in private."

As Lisa confusingly looked at Helen who also shrugged her shoulders in cluelessness, she grabbed her things just in case she wasn't coming back to her counter. The only time a supervisor took them off of the floor was an emergency meeting or a termination. She knew she hadn't done anything wrong, but perhaps she used something on a client's face that caused an allergic reaction. She definitely couldn't afford to lose her job at this point. She was barely making it with the resources that she had.

"Lisa...honey...I don't know how to say this."

"Did I do something wrong? No one recently gave me a list of allergies that they had." Lisa nervously stated.

"No...no. It's not that. I just received a call from the police department. They said your husband was in an accident."

"Oh my gosh! Is he okay?"

"I'm not sure, dear. They wouldn't give me any details over the phone."

"Oh, okay. Well, I'll call to see if he's okay."

"Uh...I think it may be best if you leave."

Lisa couldn't be sure, but it seemed as if Ms. Greene knew more than what she was telling. She immediately grabbed her things and went out to the car. She tried to call her brother in law, but she didn't get an answer. Instead of calling Terry's parents, she called the local hospital to see if Terry was in surgery or had a room. After the hospital was unable to provide her with any sufficient information, she called his mother.

"Hello, Mrs. Adams. I normally wouldn't bother you but I received a call at work-"

"He's dead, Lisa....he's dead."

Chapter 3

Hearing that her husband had died was a hard blow to the stomach. Never in a million years did she think she'd be a widow at 26. How could such a horrible thing have happened to her? Sure the argued and she thought about divorce, but she hadn't considered that he'd just be taken away from her without any options. Lisa loved her husband. She couldn't keep the hot tears from running down her cheeks as she headed to the hospital for more information.

Once Lisa arrived, the hospital officials escorted her down to the morgue. It was there where she saw Terry's parents waiting by a door in the middle of the hall. She slowly walked over to her grieving in-laws. Instead of ignoring her as his mother normally would, she embraced Lisa with a howling cry. Lisa wasn't sure what to do. She never had gotten this type of reaction from her. She intimately wrapped her arms around the wailing woman. It wasn't long before Terry's dad joined the embrace.

"I...I can't believe that this happened." He began, stammering over his words. "Its like I blinked my eye and he...he vanished. It was literally a freak accident!" He squealed, unable to hold his composure.

Terry's mom instantly grabbed her husband who was now kneeling on the floor. It was obvious that they were too distraught to give any details. The hospital officials that were still patiently waiting by the door had turned the knob and quietly opened it so Lisa could enter.

"Excuse me, Darcy. This is Mr. Adams's wife." The official explained.

"Thank you, I'll take it from here. Hello, Ms. Adams. Like they said, my name is Darcy and I kind of take care of things down here. It's actually Doyle and I, but he isn't here today."

Lisa was thrown off by Darcy's hardened tone. Darcy was a small white woman with a brunette ponytail pulled towards the back. She walked as if one leg was slightly shorter than the other and her voice sounded like a fifty-year-old male smoker.

"Normally, if the patient is married we wait for the spouse to identify the body. However, since the father was already on site, he was obviously able to confirm who he was and what happened. You can choose to see him, but I will warn you that it's pretty gruesome. The father said that a two-hundred-pound crane dropped from over his head. The injuries are very much consistent."

Lisa stood frozen with her hands over her mouth for several minutes. Could she really stomach seeing her husband like this? Surely this image would be etched in her mind for eternity. She didn't want to remember Terry this way. She just couldn't.

"The mortician will fix him up as much as they can. It's ultimately up to the spouse in regards to what type of funeral that will be given. From my personal perspective, I recommend a closed casket."

"God! Would you stop for one damn second from telling me how terrible it is!" Lisa yelled.

"Ma'am, I am sorry. I'm not trying to be abrasive. This is an everyday occurrence for me. You don't know how often I hear people say that they regret seeing their loved one after a tragedy. It seriously haunts some people till death."

Lisa took Darcy's advice and walked out of the room. By the time she was out in the hall, Terry's parents had left. Part of her understood them being distraught, but what about her? She'd been with this man daily since they first started dating. Perhaps it was all an act. Maybe they wanted her to think he was dead, so he could be out of her life for good. Besides, they hated her anyway.

Lisa walked back into the room and headed towards Darcy. It was apparent to Darcy what she wanted since there would be no other reason to reenter the room. Darcy walked over to the corpse and slowly pulled the covering back.

Lisa quickly turned her head at the sight of her husband's disfigured face. She ran over to the nearest trash can and vomited. Although his appearance was horrendous, she could definitely tell that it was her husband. Regretting her decision, she staggered from the room.

A few days later, Terry's parents called Lisa regarding his funeral arrangements. They told her that they would handle all financial obligations for the ceremony. Terry's mother mentioned to Lisa that she should come by and sign some papers that would exclude her from any cost. Although she verbally agreed to, Lisa never did. The last person she wanted to see was Terry's dad who carried all of Terry's physical features. Besides, this was their only time calling her since the accident. They didn't even ask how she was doing. Even though it was a heart-wrenching decision, Lisa also decided that she wasn't going to attend the funeral.

Chapter 4

A few days after Terry's funeral, Lisa was contacted by a lawyer. The lawyer told her that she needed to come to the office to sign off on some documents involving Terry. Lisa was confused because she was unaware that they had a lawyer. They could barely afford their regular bills, how could he pay to have a lawyer? Then, it dawned on Lisa that this had to be Terry's mother's doing.

Lisa figured that his mother was trying to put Terry's truck in her name. She couldn't afford anything extra with what she was making. She didn't even know how she was going to afford the rental. Lisa wasn't going to go out without a fight. She called Helen whose cousin was a legal aid. For a hundred dollars, he agreed to act as her attorney.

It was the day of the meeting and Lisa walked into the lawyer's office with confidence. James, Helen's cousin, suggested that he do all the talking. They were escorted into a conference room where Terry's parents were already waiting. Trying to be cordial, Lisa said hello but they didn't respond.

"Hello, everyone," the lawyer said as he walked in. "My name is John Hue and I represent Mr. and Mrs. Adams, Terry's parents.

"Hello, I am Lisa, Terry's wife. We spoke over the phone. This is my attorney James Kline."

"When did you get a lawyer?" Mrs. Adams asked with a frown.

"I take it there are some documents that you would like my attorney to review," Lisa said, ignoring Terry's mother as she did her earlier.

"Is this legal?" Mrs. Adams asked John Hue.

"Uh...yes. Ms. Lisa does have a right to counsel," he responded, clearing his throat while handing James the paperwork. "As you can see, all joint accounts will now be left to Lisa with the exception of the truck loan. Any balances that have accumulated will be brought to a zero balance out of courtesy of my clients."

"You said with exception of the truck loan, right?" Lisa asked.

"Correct. My clients have agreed to pay off the vehicle debt with the terms that the truck will stay with them. Also, since there are no kids involved, my clients would like you out of their duplex within the next sixty days."

"Are you serious? How am I supposed to live?" Lisa objected.

"My clients are offering you twenty-five thousand dollars upon your departure and the signing of these documents today."

Lisa and James looked at one another. In Lisa's peripheral vision, she could see Mrs. Adams who was intensely looking at James. As James continued to read through the documents, Terry's mother seemed to get more nervous the further he got along.

"Look, Mr. Adams and I don't have all day. We just lost our son and we would like to put an end to this as quickly as possible, so we can properly grieve. We'll offer fifty thousand and that's the deal. Take it or leave it now!" She urged.

Her sense of urgency only raised suspicion as Lisa turned to James who actually began to chuckle. According to Terry, his parents weren't willing to give him a dime as long as it involved Lisa. There had to be some other reason why his mother was so hasty for her to sign those papers.

"I can't believe you guys," James said. "This poor woman just lost her husband and you guys are trying to swindle her out of five hundred thousand dollars."

"What?" Lisa questioned.

"According to these documents that I'm assuming John Hue drafted, if you sign these documents, you won't be able to get compensation from the insurance policy that they had for their son. It clearly entitles you, the married entity, to this payment."

"That's bullshit!" Mrs. Adams yelled. "She didn't love my boy. She wouldn't even give him kids."

"Regardless of their marital issues, Mrs. Adams, my client is entitled to this payment."

"She verbally agreed that she would sign the papers if we paid for the cost of the funeral."

"Mrs. Adams, even a recorded verbal agreement to sign papers that hadn't been seen is inadmissible in court."

"She didn't even attend his funeral!" Mrs. Adams cried out loud.

"Again, a personal decision of my client," James argued.

"Greg! Do something!" Mrs. Adams pleaded to her husband.

The entire opposing party knew that there was nothing that they could do. Terry's parents clearly didn't expect for Lisa to have backup. They intended to sell her on twenty-five thousand dollars and be done with her for good. However, the universe was definitely in Lisa's favor. She walked out of the office five hundred thousand dollars richer.

Even though Terry's parents tried to get over on Lisa, she still respected two of their wishes. She gave them their son's truck and she moved from their duplex a month and a half sooner than expected. Living in that home alone was torture, so she was happy to oblige her former in laws. Lisa had enrolled herself into counseling since it was difficult to cope, but she stopped going only a few months after. She also increased Helen's cousin payoff to a cool ten thousand dollars. Had he not been there, she knew she would have not thoroughly read those documents.

Lisa found her an upscale gated community in the city. It came with three luxurious lap pools, a full workout gym, marble floors, thousands of square feet, and a personal hot tub on her balcony. She started buying high quality video equipment and recording makeup tutorials from her home. It wasn't long before she was getting paid a significant amount of money from her tutorials and Macy's became a thing of the past. Her new life was simply amazing. Although she was still at times distressed about what happened to her late husband, she wasn't sure if she'd change anything.

Chapter 5

Staying in an upscale neighborhood introduced Lisa to a lot of interesting people. Like most nosey women, they wanted to know how someone so young and single was able to afford to stay there. Lisa had no desire to share her full story with strangers, so she simply told people she was divorced. She also took pride in letting people know about her tutorials. When people saw her videos and how many subscribers she had, they no longer had any reason to question her authenticity.

Lisa hadn't been out in a while, so when Bethany, her next door neighbor, asked her to come to a country club party, she agreed. Bethany was a gorgeous Latina woman with long, flowing locks of dark hair. You could tell by her tiny, muscular physique that she was a fitness guru. Also a divorcee, Bethany was part owner of two Gold's Gyms in a nearby area.

"You look gorgeous, mommy," Bethany said as Lisa met her in the lobby.

Lisa had on a fitting black dress with matching red bottom shoes. Her natural curls were pinned up with few loose flowing strings. She came alone just in case she decided to leave if she wasn't having a good time. Once Lisa walked into the main room, she was astonished by lavish designs and luxury seating. She followed Bethany to a table where expensive bottles of champagne were waiting on ice. After the waiter came by and popped a bottle, the fun began.

After several glasses of champagne, the ladies went to the dance floor to cut a rug. Lisa was having so much fun that she didn't notice the man that was eye-balling her the entire night. However, once Bethany brought him to her attention, Lisa felt a bit of anxiety come over her.

Lisa didn't want to act as if she was stuck up, so she made flirtatious jokes about how she'd have him wrapped around her finger. She honestly hadn't been interested in dating since her late husband's accident. She knew at some point she would have to move on, but she wasn't sure if it was right then. She gave Bethany an excuse to leave and left the party. She just wasn't ready to date again.

About a week later, Lisa got a knock at her door. A delivery man had a dozen of red roses and the same expensive champagne bottle that she had at Bethany's party. Attached were a card and a phone number that said 'Please call me so I can properly ask you out'. Lisa felt a type of way about a stranger having her address. It was no secret where he had gotten the information from. She marched right over to Bethany's apartment.

"Did you enjoy your beautiful surprise?" Bethany asked after opening the door.

"Uh...not so much. I'm not comfortable with a stranger having my address when you know that I obviously live alone." Lisa straight-forwardly responded.

"Lisa, don't worry. Trevor wouldn't harm a butterfly. Besides, he doesn't know exactly where you stay. I told the guy at the gate to buzz me when the delivery man came."

"Well...I guess I feel a little better. How well do you know him?"

"He's my ex-husband cousin's best friend. He's an entrepreneur who helps small businesses with profit losses. His last girlfriend cheated on him, so he's currently single with no kids."

"I don't know, Bethany. I mean...he's handsome, but I've never really dated outside my race before."

"What do you mean? He is Afro-Latino. That means he's black!" Bethany laughed.

"What's his personality like?"

"He's very laid back and introverted until he gets to know you. He'll literally have you laughing until your stomach hurts."

"Okay... maybe I'll consider hanging out if you could set up a group thing."

Two weeks after their conversation, Lisa met with Bethany, Trevor and a few other friends. It wasn't long before she and Trevor went out on a date alone. He was just as charming and humorous as Bethany had said he was. About two months or so later, they were officially a couple.

Trevor wasn't afraid to show Lisa his adventurous side. They went biking, hiking, indoor mountain climbing, and did several other outdoor activities. Lisa was so intrigued by this man that she secretly started taking Spanish lessons. She was happy that she finally allowed herself to open up and receive love. Sure enough, after a year and a few months, Lisa became Mrs. Lisa Adams Lopez. Lisa knew that life couldn't get any better than this.

Chapter 6

Now that they were married, Lisa and Trevor decided that buying a home would make more sense than renting. Today was the day that they were meeting with a real estate agent to look at houses. Lisa wanted a minimum of five bedrooms for their new home, but Trevor wanted no more than three. This made Lisa wonder about Trevor's views about having kids in a few years.

As Lisa stood in the bathroom getting ready, several thoughts began to cross her mind about being childless. Lucky for her, Trevor was not in a hurry to have kids either. His perspective was that newlyweds should get the most out of each other as possible. Despite her initial decision to hold off on having kids, Lisa had been getting a slight touch of baby fever lately. It seemed like everyone in her new circle had a kid.

"Trevor, I know we agreed that we should hold off on kids, but I'm starting to think that this may be a good time to consider it. I don't want to end up in my mid thirties trying to have our first child."

"You want to have a kid now?" He asked, entering into the bathroom.

"Not today, but I think it would make more sense to get more bedrooms on the front end. I don't plan on moving from our house a year or so after we get it."

"Lisa, you're not even thirty yet. Don't worry. There will be plenty of time to have kids. As a matter of fact, why don't we practice," he teased, placing his hand between her thighs.

He slowly inched up to her vagina and began to caress the outside of her panty line. He slid off her silk underwear as she turned around to face his seduction. Placing her on the bathroom counter, he stretched out her legs before sliding out his nine-inch hardness. He eased inside her wetness with a deep pump. She moaned in pleasure as he gripped her ass cheeks and increased the momentum of his deep thrust.

Lisa clamped her legs around his body so that she could feel every inch inside of her. Overwhelmed by the tingling sensation between her thighs, she grabbed his head and placed it in her bosoms while he instinctively licked her jiggling nipples. As soon as she climaxed, the warm juices from his body exploded inside her womb.

After their short afternoon lovemaking session, they quickly washed up so they could meet their agent on time. Bethany's sister suggested the agent that helped them purchase their home a few months ago. He lived in an entirely different area code, but he was highly recommended.

Lisa and Trevor arrived around outside a grand house about forty-five minutes from town. The relocation aspect was no problem since they both could practically do their work from anywhere. A sexy, black man in dress pants and a tie stepped outside of a black Lexus. He said his name was Bryson Alexander as he greeted Trevor first and then smiled at Lisa with his gorgeous white teeth. Lisa could have sworn there was a little wink in his eye, but she couldn't tell. Lucky for her, Trevor wasn't an insecure man.

Bryson had set up four different homes for them to see. During the third viewing, Trevor explained that he had an important unexpected business meeting and they couldn't see the fourth house. Bryson explained it would be a while before he could reschedule the viewing, so he suggested that Lisa still come and take pictures. After they were all in agreement, Lisa followed Bryson to the next home.

"Now this is a six bedroom, newly renovated home. I'm thinking it may be a little too much home for just the two of you."

"Well... I kinda want kids in the next two years, so six wouldn't be too much. Besides, I'm sure my mom and Trevor's mom would like to come and stay with us once the baby is here."

"Oh, I see. Well, I hope I'm not out of line but it seems as if he is the luckiest man in the world to have a woman...I'm sorry...a wife as beautiful as you."

"Thanks." Lisa replied without a smile, not wanting to show any interest.

"I mean...I'm no one's judge, but I wouldn't leave my beautiful wife for a pop-up business call. I personally would have said that I have plans with my wife today, so call back tomorrow."

"Yeah, but I guess that's why each man has his own relationship to attend to."

"You are certainly right, Mrs. Lopez. Forgive me if you thought I was intruding."

Perhaps this agent was being sincere or either he was trying to find cracks in their foundation. Either way, Lisa wasn't falling for his antics. She loved her husband no matter how handsome the next guy was. However, although she would never let Bryson know, he did have a point. *What kind of meeting did Trevor have that would immediately require him to leave?*

Chapter 7

Two months after meeting Bryson, Lisa and Trevor were having their first house-warming party. Bryson brought by an elegant floor plant along with a gorgeous date to the event. Lisa couldn't figure out if he had a girlfriend all along or if he brought her to make it seem as if his previous statements were innocent. Lisa didn't have time to figure out this man's questionable behavior. She was too busy trying to figure out why Trevor had been so tired and distant lately.

Halfway into the party Trevor was missing in action. He hadn't told her that he was leaving and his car was still in the garage, so Lisa knew he was there. She moved about the party like everything was normal. Just as she was about to go upstairs, one of Trevor's guests stopped her.

"Hey, Lisa. Do you remember me from the wedding?"

"Uh...yeah. Your Trevor's niece, right?"

"No, I'm his cousin, Summer. Everyone used to think that we were twins back in the day."

"Oh okay. Nice to see you again. Enjoy the party," Lisa said, trying to get back to her mission.

"Oh...I...was...uh...gonna ask you about your landscape outside. Who does your gardening? It's beautiful!"

"It was like this when we bought it."

"Do you plan on hiring a gardener to keep it maintenance? We have a cousin named Zeus that does a terrific job with flowers and such. He definitely has a green thumb."

"Oh okay. Trevor and I may take you up on your offer," Lisa said, trying to walk away again.

"If it's not too much," the cousin swiftly intervened in Lisa's tracks, "could I give you a little insight on these particular flower bushes that you have in your yard? I remember Zeus showing me how to keep them looking magnificent all year round."

Lisa didn't want to be rude to Trevor's cousin. She was nice and polite, but she seemed to be purposely distracting her. Perhaps she was just trying to create a common interest between them, so they could bond. Lisa skeptically obliged Summer's request and went outside.

Surprisingly this woman seemed to know a lot about flowers. She knew the names of the different plants and how to treat them. Lisa pretended to take notes in her phone, but she was actually googling whatever Summer said. Turns out this lady wasn't stalling after all.

By the time they came back into the house, Trevor was in the main room mingling with the guest. Since everyone was around and having a good time, she decided to wait until she questioned him. She wondered, *was it just her or did he seem more relaxed?*

Later that night, Trevor fell asleep early after taking several shots with his friends and family. Lisa was upset because she didn't get a chance to talk to him. Deciding not to push the issue, she too got ready for bed. After putting on her silk gown and placing a satin cap over her curls, Lisa heard Trevor's phone ding. She normally would pay it no mind, but her intuition told her to look at it. She picked it up from the end table and saw that a photo had been sent to him.

Lisa opened the photos and saw several pictures of Trevor and his cousins having a good time. Some of the photos were from the party and others appeared to be old photos taken before they met. She almost felt crazy entertaining her own thoughts. Just as she was about to click off the photos, another message came through. Lisa read the message of some woman named Jasmine who was professing her erotic desires for her husband.

Two weeks had passed and Lisa still hadn't mentioned to her husband what she saw in his phone. She had sent the pictures to her phone and permanently deleted everything from Trevor's phone, so he wouldn't know that his messages were read. Trevor was always doing business for restaurants, so some groupie waitress could've gotten a hold of his number. Either way, Lisa was going to do more investigating before overreacting.

After Trevor left for work one morning, Lisa decided to call Summer over, so she could help with a few things in the yard. She had been doing some decorating as well and wanted Summer's input since she was so crafty outside. She had photos and picture frames out in the living room in order to get some opinions about the best ones.

An hour later, Summer showed up in a white t-shirt and shorts. She also had her sun glasses and hat as if she was ready to work. The ladies went out in the yard, pulled a few weeds and planted a few new flowers.

"Come on in the house," Lisa said, wiping the sweat from her forehead, "I'll make us some lemonade."

"I see everything is coming along great," Summer said, looking at the new decorations.

"Thank you. Trevor wanted me to put a few pictures up of the family in the living room. Which ones do you like best?" Lisa asked, entering the room with their drinks.

"Wow! These are so gorgeous. These are from the house warming party, aren't they? They came out great!"

"Yeah. I especially like the one where you, Molly, Trevor, and Ricky were taking shots."

"Molly?"

"Yeah. You all are in a couple of photos together."

Summer looked at the pictures and laughed. "No, mamacita, that's our cousin, Jasmine."

Lisa looked at Summer who was drinking her lemonade as if nothing was wrong. *Did she just say Jasmine?* Lisa quickly slammed down her drink and with her arm, pinned Summer to the couch by her neck.

"What type of fuckin' game are you and Trevor playing?"

"Hey! Get off of me! What are you talking about?"

Lisa pulled the phone from her pocket and showed Summer the text. The expression on Summer's face was guilt. She immediately started apologizing.

"I'm so sorry," she cried. "Trevor's ex moved back in town and he couldn't shake off his love for her. Trevor begged me to lie about who she was so-"

"You two had the balls to bring this bitch into my house and pretend like she's your cousin!"

"I'm sorry, but Trevor made me-"

"Get the fuck out of my house!"

Summer ran out of the living room door in tears. Lisa couldn't believe the fuckery that she had endured. *Did her husband and Jasmine sneak off and have sex in their home when he was missing in action?* Lisa hit the wall as tears of her husband's betrayal flowed down her cheeks.

Chapter 8

A month had gone by and Trevor continued to send apology notes, flowers, and whatever gifts his money could buy. After Lisa kicked him out and built a fire pit out of his clothes, he'd been staying at his aunt's spare condo. He claimed that he and Jasmine were together before they even started dating. Jasmine came back in town a few months ago and reached out to him.

Trevor went on to say that he said he explained to Jasmine that he was married and that she needed to move on with her life. He also went on to say that the only reason Jasmine was at the party was because Summer had brought her there unknowingly to him. Trevor's claims were that he never slept with Jasmine and didn't have any intentions on trying to rekindle anything with her.

Although Lisa felt like he wasn't telling the entire truth, she really did miss him. She was on her second marriage and she really wanted it to work. Once again, she confided in her mom who told her that everyone deserved a second chance. Lisa took her mother's advice and reluctantly allowed him back home in order to try and work things out for the sake of the marriage.

It didn't take long for Trevor to get back into the habit of his mysterious ways. He'd supposedly work longer hours and grew more resistant to his wife's sexual needs. Trevor said he was trying to establish early retirement for the both of them. However, according to their bank records Trevor was spending a lot more than what he was putting in to their accounts. Enough was enough when Lisa discovered a five thousand dollar withdrawal from their account. Trevor claimed it was a loan for a cousin. Lisa was already on to how loosely Trevor and his family used the term 'cousin'. While Trevor was asleep, Lisa switched the sim cards in the phones and set up a surprise meeting with Jasmine.

Lisa had told Jasmine to meet in a private balcony area of a prestigious restaurant. She had flowers, champagne, and a candlelit dinner in order to solidify a romantic date for her and Trevor. She waited for Jasmine to arrive and get seated before going over to the table. After recognizing her from the pictures, Lisa calmly sat down.

"Hello, Jasmine. You are much prettier in person than your pictures."

"Oh my god. What the hell is this and where is Trevor?"

"Jasmine, I don't want trouble. I just want to know why my man is giving his cousin five thousand dollars while we're having a baby."

Lisa was very calculating in her approach. Just as she did Summer, she pretended as if she already knew the facts. She wanted to see how Jasmine would react if she was told that she was being presented as a cousin and her reaction to Trevor having a child. If Trevor was as much of a liar as Lisa had now presumed him to be, he was definitely telling them two different things. Based on her appearance, Jasmine didn't seem to be the type of woman who'd knowingly accept second place.

"Lisa, right? I don't have time for this. You and Trevor need to figure out your own dysfunctional problems before you come to me," Jasmine stated, getting up from the table.

"Before you go, Jasmine. I took the liberty of reversing that transaction that my husband tried to make in order to get you into therapy. I can't imagine why a pretty girl like you would get strung out on drugs, but I've definitely seen stranger things."

"Your husband? What do you mean your husband? Trevor isn't married. Trevor told me that he doesn't even believe in traditional marriage. He believes the spiritual bonding between two people should be enough."

"We've been married for about a year now, but that shouldn't come as a surprise to you since you're his cousin. He said that you begged for the money in order to rid your opioid addiction. Here is a copy of our marriage license and the transaction that I canceled. I hope you can find counseling elsewhere other than your cousin. Good day, madam," Lisa finished, pretending to get up and leave.

"Lisa, I think we both know that Trevor isn't my cousin, but he didn't tell me that he was married. He and Summer both told me that you were a clingy ex girlfriend who needed help with an addiction. That's why I'm pissed that he used that same damn story on you about me."

"So you two have clearly been sleeping together, right?"

"Of course we have. That money was supposed to be for our down payment on our house together."

Lisa was pissed beyond believe. This traitor was using their money to have an entirely separate life with someone else. The fury inside her was hard to hide. However, she managed to keep poise in front of Jasmine.

"Jasmine, for your information, I decided to work things out with my husband. Now that you know that you were dealing with a married man, hopefully you'll take heed to this warning to stay the hell out of my way."

Chapter 9

A few weeks later while in bed, Lisa couldn't help but to think about her meeting with Jasmine. She absolutely didn't believe Jasmine's story about her believing that she was a broken ex girlfriend. The event that Jasmine came to was clearly a house warming party where several guests were there, congratulating them on their homeownership. The dumbest person in the world would have seen through that. Either her ego was too big to accept the fact that Trevor was choosing another woman, or she'd do anything to continue swindling Trevor out of their money.

Lisa imagined Jasmine sitting back laughing at her while Trevor was still being her boy toy. It was her husband's fault for making her look like an idiot. Perhaps the blame was on both of them, but Lisa had plans to put a stop to everything.

"Trevor, why don't we do something adventurous to rekindle the passion we once had?"

"Lisa, what is this now? I thought we were over this miscommunication nonsense. I thought we were back on good terms."

"Yes, we are getting better, but do you remember that fire that we had when we first got together? We made love every night, sometimes two or three times."

"Lisa, every marriage experiences downtime. I don't desire you any less. I've just been working harder."

"I know you have and that's why we both need a break. Besides, I could really use some adventurous photos for my blog."

"Alright, my queen. I'll make some arrangements for us to go up to the cabins."

"That sounds great, babe! Oh…make sure that you schedule some time for us to do some river rafting. I think the adrenaline from it will have us sexing one another like rabbits."

It was finally time for their getaway and Lisa was excited about getting some new scenery. As she checked her account to make sure all of the reservation fees were paid, she noticed an extra thousand dollars missing from the account. She asked Trevor about the transaction and he told her that he withdrew cash so that they could have some money in their pocket to spend. Lisa was happy that Trevor was finally taking this much needed vacation seriously.

After a three and a half hour flight, they arrived at The Great Rapids Resort. Lisa was amazed by the sparking river and waterfalls surrounding their cabin. They had chocolate covered strawberries and wine waiting in their suite. Soft, instrumental music was playing as a light wind blew a cool breeze through the satin curtains where a lavender incense candle was lit. The ambiance alone put Lisa in the mood. Trevor said that he'd be happy to join her after a shower. Lisa stripped naked and covered herself with the white robe provided by the resort.

Instead of waiting, Lisa thought it would be spontaneous to join her husband in the shower. She eased her way into the bathroom and pulled off the fitted robe. She seductively stepped in the shower and gently grabbed Trevor's penis. She massaged it between her fingers as she fiddled around the tip. He pushed his body up against hers as he cornered her against the tile.

Trevor picked her up and positioned himself inside of her legs as if he was about to carry her. He submerged his manhood deeply inside her openness, making quick, deep thrusts. She moaned in delight as the water from the shower kept them lubricated just enough for him to slide in and out with ease. Feeling the tingling sensation getting more intense, she erupted in pleasure shortly before he came inside of her.

After their love making session, Lisa and Trevor decided to relax and have a romantic dinner by the bonfire that the resort had made outside of the restaurant. They laughed and talked about old times as if they were best friends. They played trivia and took several tequila shots with other couples who had joined the fun.

The day went exactly as Lisa had hoped it would. They both were ready for another round of passionate lovemaking as soon as they entered the suite. As Lisa patiently waited for Trevor to finish up in the bathroom, she noticed that he received a message on his phone. She walked over and saw Jasmine's name with a message that said: **Thank you Papi for the money. See you when you get back**.

Chapter 10

"Oh my god! Someone help me!" Lisa screamed as she held Trevor's bloody head.

Unfortunately, no one was around the area at that time. Lisa propped Trevor's head on the inflatable raft that they had rented earlier that day. She frantically ran to different areas as she tried to get a signal on her phone to contact the resort's main office. They were a few miles out, so she knew that she wouldn't be able to pull him in the raft on her own.

Lisa paced back and forth, trying to decide what to do. She was afraid to leave him alone in case a wild animal would come along and try to ravish his flesh. She at least had a full size paddle to scare it away from them. Lisa felt helpless as blood continued to protrude from the large gash in his head.

About thirty minutes later while Lisa continued to hold his head and attempt to dial out on her phone, a passerby found her in distress. He immediately ran up to Lisa and tried to assist her with Trevor. He bent down and checked Trevor's pulse. He looked at Lisa with the most utterly confused look that a person could give.

"How long have you guys been out here?"

"We came out here this morning. Trevor wanted to get an early start before all the other guests crowded the river?"

"How did this happen?"

"He fell out of the raft and hit his head on a rock. Please help me. We need to get his body back inside the raft."

"Uh ma'am. I'm no doctor, but...uh... I think this man is dead."

"No sir. He's my husband and he's just unconscious. Please, help me get him in the raft so that we can pull him."

"I'm not sure that's gonna work. I'll call the resort authorities instead."

Lisa watched as the stranger walked farther up the river trail to get a signal. It wasn't long before an ambulance came and tried to revive Trevor. They also looked at Lisa as if it was a hopeless situation.

"My husband is alive. You just have to keep trying. He's unconscious. He'll wake up once you put that thing on him."

"Ma'am...what thing?"

"The thing where you say 'clear' and pump his chest."

The two EMS assistants looked at one another. They were used to families being in denial about their loved ones, so they attempted to show some compassion by not covering his face. They even allowed Lisa to ride in the ambulance and hold his hand. Lisa continued to speak to him as if he was listening. Once they arrived at the hospital, they advised Lisa to wait outside.

"Do the 'clear' thing!" Lisa yelled, watching the hospital personnel take Trevor down the hall.

An hour later, the doctor came out and pulled down his mask. He walked over to Lisa with a solemn look on his face. He put his hands together as if he was about to make a momentous speech.

"Mrs. Lopez, I'm sorry. Your husband lost too much blood."

"Well, can't he get a blood transfusion?"

"No, Mrs. Lopez. I'm sorry, but he's gone."

"No! He can't be! He was breathing in the ambulance!" Lisa yelled as the tears came streaming down her face.

"Do you have someone that you can call?" The doctor asked.

"The two of us are on a romantic getaway. I just need my husband."

"I'm sorry, Mrs. Lopez." The doctor said, walking away from her.

After the funeral, Lisa spent her next two weeks in bed. She avoided all calls and didn't touch her computer. She couldn't help but to think that it was her fault that her husband was no longer with her. Had she not convinced him to go on the trip, he'd still be alive.

Moments later, Lisa heard a knock at her door. Normally she would ignore it, but the knock was kind of loud and annoying. Perhaps the resort's investors wanted to ask her more questions regarding the accident. The resort was probably afraid that Lisa would sue them. She looked out of the peephole and discovered a totally unexpected person.

"What are you doing?" She asked, keeping the chain on the door.

"Well, I heard about what happened, so I wanted to stop by and check on you."

"Well, I'm clearly not doing well. My husband just died."

"My condolences, Ms. Lopez. I know that this is a hard time and-"

Lisa immediately closed the door and locked it. She wasn't sure what Bryson's intentions truly were. Although he was their realtor, she wasn't sure if he was being sincere or trying to slide in Trevor's place. He supposedly had a girlfriend, so shouldn't he have sent a card or something instead of stopping by? This caused Lisa to consider getting extra protection since she'd be alone in her house.

About five minutes later, there was another knock at the door. Lisa's blood began to boil because she knew that it was Bryson returning. The nerve of him to keep bothering her after she clearly showed him that she wanted privacy was appalling. Without looking through the peephole, she opened the door with a swing of fierceness.

"Look, Bryson! I told you-"

"Who's Bryson?"

"Who the hell are you?" Lisa asked, staring at the short, white man in a suit.

"Oh, I'm sorry. My name is Joey. Did I catch you at a bad time?" He asked.

"I just lost my husband and I would like to grieve in peace. Am I asking too much?"

"I apologize, Ms. Lopez. That's precisely why I'm here. I wanted to go over the insurance claim regarding your husband."

"Oh."

Lisa slowly opened the door and allowed Joey to enter her home. He complemented her on the home as they walked toward the kitchen. He looked up the stairway as if she was going to turn around and lead him upstairs.

"The kitchen is this way," Lisa said, pointing straight ahead.

"Oops. No problem. It's such a nice house downstairs that a person couldn't help but to be curious about the upstairs."

Lisa didn't respond as they sat down at the table. The guy was acting so weird that she was about to ask for his credentials. He pulled out the documents that she had signed a while ago, so Lisa figured he was legit.

"Does anyone else stay here?" Joey asked.

"What difference does that make?"

"None at all. I was just asking," he responded with a nervous giggle. "Uh... was that your realtor who just left? I saw his sign on the Lexus door."

"We're doing a life insurance policy not homeowners, correct?"

"Uh...why...yes," he stammered.

"Well, why are you asking me personal questions that have nothing to do with Trevor?"

"They are just general questions, ma'am. I thought I was making conversation."

"Well, I suggest you ask me relevant questions regarding the claim before I report your unprofessionalism to the NAIC."

Joey immediately got down to business and started asking the proper questions. Lisa couldn't control her emotions as she had to walk him through the entire ordeal again. Joey seemed to have a little more compassion by asking her did she need a minute. After everything was settled in stone, Lisa's payout was $750,000.

Chapter 11

A year later, Lisa had moved to a different state to start a new life. She and Trevor traveled often and went to plenty of social events, so she didn't want to visit the same places and see the same people from their circle. She even fell off with Bethany who kept her own distance after the accident. It almost felt as if their circle was blaming her for what happened even though they didn't bluntly come out and say it.

Lisa reached out to Bryson who helped her sell the home that he helped them to purchase. She broke even in the sell for the most part, but that was okay with her. After spending quite a bit of time working with Bryson on the selling of the home, they became close. He was there for her like a best friend. It was only natural that they also became lovers.

The people in her town were infuriated when they heard about the relationship. They called her a backstabbing whore for getting with the realtor. Lisa didn't understand what all the hate was about. It wasn't like Trevor and Bryson were best friends. He came to one house warming party, for Christ's sake. Lisa even had to temporarily shut down her blog from all of the backlash that she received. It seemed to her that people wanted her to be miserable and a widow forever. She couldn't understand why people refused to accept the fact that she was happily in love again.

"Bryson, I know you said that you wanted a big wedding, but I think we should have something small, you know...kind of intimate."

"What do you mean? All of my fraternity brothers are prepared to get their suits. The bachelor party is set, and we've already got the venue rented."

"I know, but think of how much money we'll save if we go down to the courthouse and then have a big reception."

"Lisa, we're not hurting for money. We still have over half a million in our account."

"I know we're not hurting for money. I was just saying that maybe-"

"Lisa, I realize that you've been married twice already. I get it. Perhaps a third wedding is overwhelming. But I'm not cutting myself short just because you had double failures."

"Hey! That's an asshole thing to say!"

"I'm sorry, baby. Look, I didn't mean to upset you. I just want to share one of the most important days of my life with the most important people in my life. Is that too much to ask?"

Lisa looked at Bryson who seemed to be sincere in his approach. Although she didn't want to argue about money, it was definitely part of the problem. He didn't know about the settlement that Lisa received from her first marriage, but he was aware of the second policy that she received. He even suggested that they take a million dollar life insurance policy out on each other. Lisa wasn't opposed to it, but she wondered what prompted him to suggest it.

The main issue that Lisa had with Bryson was finances and inconsistency. Ever since they had moved in together, Bryson had slacked up on his real estate business. He went from being number one in his district to selling one house a month. He told Lisa that his real passion was renovating homes and that he wanted them to start their own business together. She believed in his dream and put $75,000 in as a down payment to get what he needed. He bought a used pickup truck and $15,000 worth of power tools. Other than that, the other $40,000 was unaccounted for.

After six months of compromising, they settled on a small wedding in the islands with close family and friends. The wedding package cost half of what they had originally planned and Bryson got the ceremony that he wanted. Lisa was glad to see him happy after the frightening episodes he'd been having lately. A few weeks ago, he had grabbed her by the neck and slammed her against the wall when she had asked about the missing money she had loaned him. He apologized and said that he was under a lot of stress. His apology had seemed sincere until he slapped her across the face two days prior to the wedding for going through his phone. Again, he apologized but said it was her fault for invading his privacy.

It didn't take long for the abuse to escalate. Sometimes he'd come home, reeking of alcohol, and pick a fight with her for no apparent reason. Lisa would fight back, but ultimately, Bryson would over power her. She'd have bruises all over her body with the exception of her face.

It was Saturday morning and Lisa had been feeling tired the entire week. Bryson had been gone more than he had been there, so that gave her a bit of relief. She started feeling nauseous after eating her normal breakfast, which was certainly unusual. It didn't take long for Lisa to realize that she had forgotten to make her appointment for her depo shot. Panicked, she checked her phone calendar to see what date she was due to have it. Lisa went over by three weeks.

That afternoon, Bryson came home with a smile on his face for a change. He was dressed in his real estate attire, which was something he hadn't done in a while. He set his briefcase on the table and said that he had good news. Although Lisa wasn't feeling well, she still pretended to be excited. She was feeling perplexed because she had taken a pregnancy test and it had come back positive.

"Baby, I have some great news. My business partner and I bought a unit to remodel and we're going to fix it up and sell it for double the money!"

"That sounds great, love. I'm so happy for you."

"I couldn't have done it without you," he said, kissing her on the head. He gently grabbed her breast and started kissing her neck. "Let's celebrate," he continued, putting his hand between her legs.

"Sweetheart, I'm not feeling well. Let's wait until tonight when I'm feeling better."

"What do you mean you're not feeling well? Oh...you think I'm stupid. You think that I don't know. Someone else has been in my pussy, huh?"

"Bryson, don't be crazy. No one-"

He instantly grabbed her and slammed her down on the couch from behind. She had been lounging around all day, so she only dressed in a t-shirt and underwear. It was obvious what his intentions were.

"Bryson! Stop! What are you doing?"

Ignoring her plea, he snatched off her panties and put himself inside of her. "I'll show you crazy." He said, aggressively plunging in and out of her vagina while grabbing a fistful of her curls.

After he was done, he got up, went to the bathroom, and left the house. He didn't even check to see if she was okay. Lisa was stunned. Although he didn't physically hurt her, she was emotionally and mentally torn. Out of all people in the world, her own husband had basically raped her.

Chapter 12

Knowing that he had done wrong, Bryson hadn't been home for over two weeks. He had his sister, Angela call Lisa and plead his case. His sister had told Lisa that Bryson had gotten back addicted to cocaine. She explained that when their father died six years ago, Bryson had gotten strung out on drugs. Two years later, he cleaned himself up and became a successful realtor.

Angela figured that Bryson was recalling the father and son talks that he had with his dad. He probably didn't imagine that his dad would be absent from one of the most important times in his life. Bryson's parents had been married for over 40 years, so marriage was sacred to him. Angela couldn't be certain that this alone had triggered it, but Bryson had obviously relapsed for some unknown reason.

Lisa agreed to accept Bryson back on the condition that he put himself back into rehab. Bryson happily agreed and immediately enrolled in the program. After four weeks of going hard and motivation from his wife, Bryson was again drug free. He was back to being the loving, sincere, and passionate husband that he once was. When he was finally able to stay home for good, Lisa surprised him with a **Welcome home, you're gonna be a DAD**! banner.

Six months had passed and Lisa was almost eight months pregnant. Everything was going perfect and they had just finished designing the nursery. They found out at their reveal party that they were going to be the happy parents of a baby girl. Bryson seemed more excited than Lisa was. This was the life that Lisa dreamed of having.

"Hey, hubby!" Lisa gleefully said as Bryson walked through the door.

Lisa quickly noticed that his energy didn't match. He seemed down and oppressed. Lisa nervously watched him as he sat down at the kitchen island.

"Is everything okay, babe?" She softly asked.

"I just got a call from the guy who was supposed to sell us the unit. After all that fucking work that we put into the units, they reneged on the loan, saying that we were unable to meet proper deadlines."

"They can't do that to you. You had to stop working for health reasons. Don't worry, babe, we'll get a lawyer and figure it out." Lisa said.

"It's no need. We already signed it back over and they paid us for most of our work."

"It's okay, babe. We'll find something bigger and better."

"Thanks, babe."

Bryson gave Lisa a kiss on the stomach and left the house. She wanted to stop him, but she was afraid that his disappointment and frustration may trigger him to get angry. The last thing she needed was an episode while she was this far along in her pregnancy. She called his sister and told her to keep an eye on him.

It was almost one in the morning and Lisa had wakened from hearing Bryson walk through the door. Her heart began beating fast as she listened to his staggering footsteps from the bedroom. He came in, turned on the light, and grabbed her arm.

"Lisa, I need you to go to this address and get my package."

"Bryson, what are you talking about? It's one in the morning!"

He quickly slapped her over the face. " I don't care what fucking time it is, go get my shit!"

"I'm eight months pregnant, Bryson," Lisa cried out. "What do you mean? Go and get what?"

"I don't give a fuck about that. You didn't think about being eight months pregnant when you ran your mouth to my sister. Now, my guy won't give me what I need, so you're gonna go get it!"

Looking at the hatred in his eyes, Lisa knew that he was serious. Not wanting to risk her health or the baby's, she got up and dressed herself as he told her. She took the information from him and headed to the address.

Once she arrived, shivering and trying to wipe her face, she rang the doorbell to the stranger's house. A large black man in a black jumpsuit came to the door. He looked at her and giggled.

"I'm sorry, ma'am. Are you lost?"

"Uh...no. I'm here to see Skittles."

The large man looked her over and quickly pulled her in the door. He promptly closed it and put a gun to her head.

"Are you working for the fucking feds?"

Lisa had never been as frightened as she'd ever been in her life. She opened up her coat and showed her belly. The guy took the gun from her head, but still held it loosely in his hand.

"What happened to your eye?" He asked.

Lisa couldn't speak. She instantly started crying and slipped back on the door onto the floor. The guy put his gun away and helped her up from the floor.

"Listen, I apologize but you never can be too careful. But one thing I don't condone is beating women, especially when they're pregnant. I know off the T. O. P. this shit ain't even for you. This guy is a fucking coward, man. I can't believe a nigga would send out his pregnant woman. He must be broke and you got all the money, huh?"

Lisa shook her head in agreement.

"That's a pitiful ass dude. You know what? I got just the thing for whoever he is. Wait right here."

The man went to the back and came back up front a few minutes later. He had two separate bags in his hands. He held them up in front of Lisa.

"I want you to give him this for his little problem. But this other bag is for when he put his hands on you again. Mix that shit in his drink, but don't mix them together."

Lisa paid him the money and promptly left his house. She sat in her car and cried harder than she had ever before. *What if the man had mistaken her for a snitch and killed her*. How could her husband be so cruel? Lisa knew that the abuse would only get worse. She knew that she had to do something. She couldn't keep sacrificing herself and her baby for her husband's weaknesses. Against the dealer's warning, Lisa poured both contents together in one bag.

Chapter 13

Due to the horrific events that took place the night before, Lisa didn't wake up until the following afternoon. Bryson had evidently slept downstairs since the opposite side of the bed was crisp and neat. She went ahead and got in the shower, trying to erase last night's events from her memory.

After her shower, Lisa carefully retreated downstairs. She was almost full term, so she couldn't move about as she once did. She rounded the corner and walked toward the kitchen. She was slightly startled when she walked in and saw her husband at the kitchen table. He must have fallen asleep after satisfying his drug craving. Lisa wasn't sure what type of mood her husband would have, so she chose not to wake him. She fixed her some toast and cereal before heading into the living room.

After watching a couple of daytime television shows, Lisa realized that Bryson hadn't gotten up from the table. She wobbled back into the kitchen and quietly stopped at the opposite end of where Bryson was sitting. He was still in the same position as he was earlier. Still not wanting to wake him, she peeked around a little further and saw what looked like dried blood coming from his nose that had dripped and dried on the table. She immediately dialed 911.

Once again, Lisa was surrounded by several police investigators who questioned her about Bryson's recent whereabouts, people he may have come in contact with, and obviously the drugs. Lisa told them that Bryson had been upset about a property deal not going well, so he left and came back a few hours later. However, she didn't let them know that she went and got the drugs. After they took her statement, they told her they would follow up if they needed more information.

Unlike Trevor's family, Bryson's family was very supportive of the misfortune of Lisa losing Bryson. They helped her with errands and housework during her final few weeks of pregnancy. Exactly three weeks after the death of her husband, Lisa had a baby girl and named her Sahara Brylina Alexander. It was the happiest day in Lisa's life. Holding her baby in her arms made her realize that this moment was what she had been missing. *Why did Bryson have to be such an asshole*, she thought as she held her baby close to her heart.

To add to Lisa's triumph, she received the million dollar life insurance policy after Bryson's death. Unlike Trevor's death, Lisa had to go through several interviews regarding Bryson's accident. They would ask her the same questions in different ways as if she was going to give a different account. It was almost like they wanted to catch her in a lie.

Lisa later learned that Bryson's business partners along with some of his family members had launched a full blown investigation regarding his death. Since Bryson was well-known in the community, he also got a lot of local publicity from the news. Lisa didn't understand why people were acting like Byson was a pillar of the community. His family knew that he did cocaine. Although she did go and get the drugs, she didn't force him to take anything.

By this time, law enforcement went after Lisa with a vengeance. They started to look into Lisa even more aggressively because they found it strange that three husbands had died while married to her. During the investigation, they found out that she couldn't have had anything to do with Terry's death. However, on her old blog where she had posted pictures of her and Trevor rafting together, they found a few inconsistencies. The place where Lisa claimed that Trevor had hit his head was much further away from the pictures that she had posted on her blog. It was all circumstantial, but the case was definitely getting a lot of attention.

Meanwhile, in the case of Bryson Alexander, the medical examiner had initially determined that Bryson had died from a cocaine overdose. However, after the autopsy results had come back, it was discovered that Bryson had a toxic mix of fentanyl, cocaine, and molly in his system. Bryson's family and friends admitted that he had done cocaine, but they had never known him to take the mixture of drugs that was found. Even with all that evidence, no one could prove that Bryson hadn't obtained and administered the drugs to himself.

Chapter 14

Three years later, Lisa was in bliss with her baby girl as she sat outside in the backyard and watched her play in her life-sized Barbie doll dream home. She had downsized to a three bedroom house about forty-five minutes away from her old home. She decided to leave relationships alone for a while and focus on raising her daughter.

Sahara was just like her dad when he was clean, full of charm, energy, and laughter. She had soft, curly hair like her mom, but her facial features strongly resembled her dad.

Looking at her made Lisa sometimes wish that things would have been different. She wished that Bryson would have stayed on track and been there to help raise their daughter. Although the drug dealer had warned her not to mix the packages, she didn't think it would kill Bryson. Her hopes were to make him feel so bad that he'd never want to do drugs again. Unfortunately, it hadn't happened that way. Lisa couldn't help but to shed a tear as she watched her beautiful baby play.

"Mommy! Mommy!" Sahara yelled, running up to her. "Why mommy cry?"

"Oh, sweetie...mommy is just happy to have such a wonderful baby."

"I no baby, mommy. I big girl," she said, spreading her arms as if she had just sprinkled magic.

"I know, Cupcake. Can mommy have a big girl hug?"

Sahara gladly squeezed her mother around her neck. After a few more hours of playing, Lisa put Sahara in her bed for a quick nap. Lisa went and grabbed some clothes from the laundry so she could do some chores as Sahara slept. Ten minutes later, three police cars swarmed her home. Lisa quickly picked up the phone and called her mom.

The police didn't allow Lisa to wait until her mom arrived. Instead, she had to wake Sahara and take her with them down to the precinct. It was there when they allowed Lisa's mom to take the baby.

"So...Ms. Adams Lopez Alexander. I'm detective Howell. What is the name that you go by these days?" He asked.

"You can call me Ms. Alexander." She responded.

"Sure. Ms. Alexander, your late husband was well-known in the community. He had a promising future, am I right?"

"Which husband, since you made it your duty to announce all three?"

"That's a good point. We can talk about all three. Now, according to reports, Mr. Adams died of a freak accident at work. My sincere condolences for that. That was a totally unexpected misfortune. However, you received a lump sum of cash as a light compensation for your loss, correct?"

"Yes."

"How much?"

"It's in the paperwork."

"Ah...yes, it is," he said, picking up the folder. "His loving parents had a policy on him that also covered his wife. How nice of them, wouldn't you say?"

"It's a matter of opinion." She dryly responded.

"Wow! You get five hundred thousand dollars and it's a matter of opinion. Okay. So with Trevor, it seems as if there was some river rafting accident, correct?"

"Correct."

"Would you like to elaborate?"

"No, I would like to get home to my baby."

"We'll get to that. Now my team discovered that you had a successful blogging site, correct?"

"Correct." Lisa responded, getting annoyed.

"We were looking at the exceptional photos that you put on the blog. Now, we were all under the impression that he hit his head shortly after you guys got out there."

"Is that something you all just assumed?" She asked.

"Well, no. The autopsy report said that he had died about an hour and a half before we got there."

"That could be accurate. I mean...I couldn't get a signal on my phone and the guy that helped us arrived about thirty or forty minutes later."

"Okay. So according to the crime scene photos, you guys were about an hour away from where you initially took the pictures. What we're trying understand is how can a dead man take pictures?"

"You guys are trying to reconstruct a scene to fit in your own recreated timeline. I don't have time for this. I need to get home to my daughter."

"Ah, yes, your daughter. She's a beauty by the way. I'm just curious about something though. What do you tell her about her father?"

"She knows that daddy went to Heaven."

"That's fair. You don't want to tell a three-year-old that her dad overdosed from the drugs that her mom bought."

Lisa's entire demeanor changed. She figured this was another senseless interrogation until he threw that in that last sentence. Perhaps he was fishing. Lisa wasn't going to freely admit anything.

"Well, what do you have to say for yourself?" The detective asked.

"I don't answer declarative statements, Detective."

"You don't have to, Ms. Alexander. You don't have to say a word at all. Mr. Gary Long has agreed to give us all the information that we need."

"I don't know a Gary Long." Lisa snapped.

"Oh, I'm sorry. You may recognize him by Skittles. That's his street name."

Lisa realized that her worse nightmare had come true. How in the hell did they find this guy? Then it dawned on Lisa that Bryson's sister knew him since she was the one who paid Skittles not to sell drugs to her brother. A damn drug dealer had snitched on her.

"I'm done speaking without my attorney." Lisa stated.

Chapter 15

During the trial, Lisa was accused of purchasing the fentanyl from the same drug dealer that her former husband Bryson had done business with. Skittles had coincidentally gotten arrested for other unrelated drug charges, but he was aware of the high profiled case regarding Bryson. In exchange for a lesser prison sentence, Skittles told them that Lisa had bought the fentanyl from him. He told them that he cautioned her not to mix the drugs. He even had a recorded video of Lisa on the outside of his property.

Lisa's lawyers argued that Skittles was a low down drug trafficker who was willing to blame anyone for his crimes except for himself. They made it a point to let the jury know that Skittles had made and provided the potent drugs to an unwilling participant who was forced to go and get them. They explained that Lisa couldn't have had knowledge of the types of drugs that were handed to her and had Skittles given Lisa regular cocaine instead of the mixture, her husband may still be alive today.

The arguments were very propelling and each side had valid points. The defense wrote Lisa off as a criminal who had gotten addicted to making a living off of insurance policies. Surprisingly in her defense, Angela testified that Lisa had left her brother who begged to come back home to her. Unfortunately, the prosecution brought up the fact that Lisa had lied about buying the drugs. They also reiterated the fact that she was told not to mix them.

Lisa stuck to her claim that she was a victim of circumstances. She said that she couldn't help the fact that her three husbands happened to die in unfortunate occurrences. Also, she explained that her latest husband was addicted to drugs and was a wife beater, which was Skittles' testimony as to why he gave her the mixture.

Investigators weren't able to confirm that she killed her second husband Trevor, but they assumed that she hit him over the head with a blunt forced object and staged the river rafting scene. Although this information wasn't allowed to be entered into the trial, Lisa was still sentenced to fifteen years in prison for her participation in distributing deadly drugs to her former husband.

The insurance company was able to recoup only half of the settlement since the other half covered baby Sahara. Lisa still had an ample amount of cash saved from her other two policies as well. Using that cash flow, Lisa hired two new lawyers to work her case. After two appeals, Lisa's sentence was reduced to seven years. She got out in four for good behavior and was able to reunite with seven-year-old Sahara.

From the Author

"Thank you for taking the time to read I'm a Victim of Circumstances. I look forward to providing you with future entertainment that you will enjoy."

AND PLEASE...

If you'd like more quality fiction at this low price, I'd really appreciate a review on Amazon. The number of reviews a book accumulates on a daily basis has a direct impact on how it sells, so just leaving a review, no matter how short, helps make it possible for me to continue to do what I do. Here's a link to leave a review. Thank you in advance!

Customer Review

Feel free to check out the entire series as well as other books also available on Amazon.

Partially Broken Never Destroyed Complete Series

We Were Still Kids

The Doctor's Inn: A Private Practice

A Crime for Two

Alyce Leaves Wonderland

After Dawn Breaks

www.imadethebook.com

Unlawful Vows (Sample)

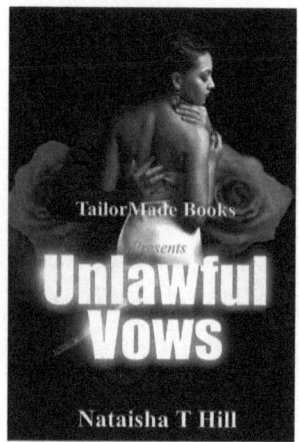

"One less filth in the world," Sandra mumbled as she trembled so hard that it seemed the four walls of the basement were spinning around her. *Or were they*? She couldn't tell. She could only tell of the tremor inside of her. Her heart rocked in her chest, as though she'd been in a death race. She was visibly shaking. If she grasped an object, it would slither from her grasp and crash down into the floor. She was that unsettled.

Her hair, honey brown and wavy, was drenched with the sweat dripping down her caramel skin. If she wasn't stark naked, her clothes would be just as wet as her hair. It had been days since she last felt the comfort of clothes. At least proper ones. Lately, she was forced to go on without clothes, and when 'they' did let her get dressed, they only provided her with clothes that fuelled their sexual perversion. Vulnerability to the harshness of the extreme weather was nothing new to Sandra at this point.

It didn't matter that she'd been forced to forgo her skincare regimen for many weeks at a stretch. Her skin still looked radiant, holding its rich caramel glow. She was the true definition of a diamond in the rough.

Her knees buckled, seeking to give way as she stood on her feet. As if that wasn't enough to drive her back to the floor, there was the painful throbbing between her legs, where the man, her so-called master, had delivered a blow with his clenched fist. Now he lay nude and motionless, his life sucked out of him. His eyes were wide open, yet seeing nothing.

They were the same eyes that had always been brimming with lust and power when he took her, tossing her back and forth like a ragged doll. It was ironic how she'd strangled him with the very same handcuffs he'd restrained her with. *Poor thing*, she thought and smirked. He definitely hadn't seen it coming. If he'd known the chains of the handcuffs would bring him to his death, he certainly would not have introduced the handcuffs into his perverted game two weeks ago.

Sandra waited for the perfect time to strike. She waited for a moment when he approached her alone, with his wife nowhere in sight. Glancing at the dead man, her eyes were frantic to find the key to the handcuffs. Sandra had found it resting on his chest where it doubled as a pendant. She crouched beside him, yanked the key off his neck and unlocked the cuffs. The cuffs fell to the floor, clanking loudly. She bristled. That was way louder than it should be. She could only hope her boss's wife hadn't heard it.

Careful not to make a sound, she advanced toward the exit, but her plan to be silent was defeated when she mounted the stairs leading out of the basement. The wooden stairs, old and rickety, creaked with each step she took. Without the death sting of iron around her wrists, her skin could finally breathe again. *Freedom, Sandra. That's the smell of freedom.*

Sandra breathed deeply, filling her lungs with fresh air. This air was different. It was poles apart from the stuffed air trapped in the basement, or dungeon as she liked to call it. The air in the basement was rather foul, clogged with the smell of rust, sweat and of course…sex—if sex had a smell.

Sandra had no idea what time it was or what day it was. She'd lost track of time. She barely even knew when it was morning or evening, unless her boss approached her with a derogatory greeting on his cigarette-darkened lips.

The house was quiet, as though there was no sign of life. But she had a feeling her mistress was up there in the master's bedroom. She proceeded toward the stairs leading to the bedroom. Cold sweat dripped down her hair and trailed down her spine, until it found her butt crack. The air conditioner had her perspiration drying up in no time though. Her steps were unhurried, almost soundless, as she made her way to the master's bedroom.

She pushed open the door, her eyes straining to see through the darkness of the room. Her eyes adjusted to the darkness—it was nighttime, obviously—and then her gaze settled on a bump on one side of the bed. Sandra smiled. There Marie was, having her beauty sleep.

She lay on her side, her head resting on one of the many soft pillows on the bed. She'd definitely fallen asleep with the thought that her husband was down there in the basement having his way with their sex slave. Sandra edged closer to Marie and then she halted, her eyes devouring the woman.

She had no idea of killing this one. Marie looked…innocent. Naïve even. What if just like Sandra, Marie had also been sexually enslaved to the pervert? What if their marriage was one huge lie and she also needed saving? More questions crowded Sandra's mind, and then she sat beside Marie and touched her arm through the covers under which she lay.

"Mmmh," Marie hummed, adjusting herself on the bed. "Go shower, Carl. You must stink after being in that pathetic place for hours."

Hours? Sandra wondered. This woman was clearly exaggerating. *Was she drugged*? Perhaps she was too far gone in her slumber to think right. Her husband had only been there for a few minutes. Twenty at the most. He clearly had something even more sinister going on outside of them both, but whatever. None of that mattered at the moment.

Marie was silent again. She had obviously drifted back into sleep. Sandra concluded that she'd been right to think that Marie was naïve. Couldn't she feel that her husband was gone? Couldn't she feel that the person beside her wasn't her Carl? Seriously though, couldn't she feel that something had happened to him? Wasn't there a way these people felt these things? Unless of course, the movies and books were all lying. If this was a movie, she'd definitely feel that her husband was gone. Maybe she'd suddenly feel dizzy, or feel a sharp sting or a stab in her chest. Anything.

This woman felt nothing. She lay there without a care in the world, her chest rising and falling gently as she breathed. Sandra couldn't deny that while she hated every moment with Carl, she'd always looked forward to having sex with Marie. In those few months she was locked up in the dungeon, she realized a truth about herself—one she wished she'd known sooner.

She had a soft spot for women. There was a hole in her life that could only be filled by a woman, and Marie looked perfect.

So, she bent toward Marie and kissed her ear. She ran her hand up and down Marie's arm, and then she whispered, "Come with me. Let us leave this place."

Partially Broken Never Destroyed (Sample)

Kayla's peace was short lived when Jeremy called her a week later, saying he wanted to make amends and at least be friends. He talked about the things he had done wrong and realizing the error of his ways. He offered to take her out to a friendly dinner so he could explain some of the things that took place. When she asked him why he couldn't just explain himself over the phone, he claimed that it was important to say what he had to say face-to-face. Who was he kidding? She knew what he was up to as always. His little fling didn't turn out as he expected. Although she had absolutely no intentions of getting back with him, she wanted to hear his reason for cheating.

Jeremy and she agreed to meet at one of their favorite restaurants called Parquet's. She figured she would dress sexy in order to rub in all of what he had been missing. She wore a black, off the shoulders, one-piece pantsuit with her leopard pumps that matched her leopard accessories. She still wasn't exactly sure how much information Jeremy had regarding Travis or any of what had went down. Being that it was a small town and one of his basketball friends was at the party with Richard and her, there was no telling what he knew. She arrived at the restaurant and noticed Jeremy was already there. The host directed her to his table and he was sitting there looking quite handsome with his black, short-sleeved polo shirt and dark blue jeans. He got up from the table and greeted her with a hug.

"Damn, girl, you upgraded since you left me, huh?"

"I left you? Is that how it went?" Kayla jokingly replied.

"No, I'm just talking, so what's new in your life? A new man perhaps?"

"Not really, I'm just taking some time to myself. How are you and your new? "

"What makes you think I have a new?"

"Well, there is the fact that I saw you two together one day and then you confirmed it weeks ago."

"Oh, that was nothing."

"So, you ruined something good over a tasteless female."

"It wasn't that, I was just going through some things with my dad and you and I were arguing all the time, I didn't know what to do."

"So, you figured the answer would be to have sex with another woman?"

"That's sort of what I wanted to talk to you about," he sighed and paused. By that time, the server came by to get their drinks.

"Proceed," she said, sounding a bit urgent.

"That girl claiming she is pregnant."

Kayla sat there in dead silence. She could not believe this loser was sitting here telling her he got someone pregnant. What in the hell was he thinking telling her this? As much as she convinced herself that she didn't want him anymore, knowing that he got someone pregnant burned her inside. She could feel the cruelty in her gradually increasing.

"What are you telling me this for, hell, you should've had her here instead of me since you got an extra person to feed."

"Damn, see that's why I wanted to talk to you face-to-face, because I knew if I did it over the phone, you would have just hung up. At least now I know you still care."

"Have you seriously lost your mind? Lose my number and die," she responded as she got up and left from the table not looking back.

"Kayla," he yelled as she was leaving, "KAYLA!"

She jumped in her car, pissed to the limit. She couldn't believe that whorish guy, who called himself a man, would get some random female pregnant. She started feeling even more justified about having sex with Travis. She started to think about how Jeremy would always say he would marry the woman who carried his first child. Then she started to feel nauseated by the thought that he may really love this woman and treat her right. She really couldn't understand why she was so upset. It's not as if this guy treated her like a queen or something, so why was she sweating this issue. Consumed by her thoughts as she pulled into her apartment complex, she didn't notice someone had been following her. She parked her car only to discover to the right side of her was Jeremy's truck. Jeremy had followed her home.

Panic came over her because she didn't know what to do. She pretended to fondle around in her purse until she could think of a good lie. He pretty much knew where the majority of her relatives lived, so she couldn't say it was an aunt or cousin's home. She was busted. She had practically given this mentally deranged man direction to her home. She decided not to worry since 9-1-1 was just a phone call away if he tried something.

"Oh, so you really came up," he said, as Kayla finally got out of her car.

"Yeah, and?"

"Oh, I'm not hating or anything, congratulations."

"Yeah, thanks," she dryly responded.

"It's good to see you're doing good and not being a low-life like all my other ex-girlfriends. Miss independent and I don't need anything from a man," he teased.

"Look, Jeremy, I don't know why you followed me; I said all I had to say at the restaurant."

"That's cool, are you going to invite me in so I can see how you're living?"

"This isn't the time and, plus, I have to be at work here shortly so…"

"How about I call you tonight and we can talk about it," he interrupted.

At this point, she didn't want him in her home, by any means. All she wanted was to see him leave and never return, so she agreed. Much to her surprise, he got in his truck, without any hesitation, and left. She felt relieved and overwhelmed all at once. She was so upset with herself for not going over to her mom's house or stopping by the store or something before going home. She started to wonder if she should buy a bat or something just in case. She had already been thinking of getting a gun, since she was a single female living on her own. Now that Jeremy knew where she stayed, it really wouldn't be such a bad idea.

At work, things weren't going any better. One of the day shift managers had written her up because she got a guest complaint the night before. The complaint claimed she was too slow bringing the food out and after she brought it out, it was cold. She couldn't help one of their lazy night shift cooks didn't feel like re-cleaning the grill. Then, Brandy had called out from work for some reason, so she figured she would have to listen to Rachael simplistic ass all night. One of the night managers informed her that the usual new hire trainer wouldn't be in, so she wanted her to train the new girl, Dana. It was just like them, to write her up and then need a damn favor.

Dana was a medium built chick with long curly hair and smooth brown skin. She had wide hips and a slightly cute face. Her only drawback was her legs were somewhat short, accentuating her too long torso. Kayla discovered that Dana dated one of her cousins back in the day, so the conversation they had while she was training her didn't seem awkward. Kayla told her she should come out with her and Brandy sometimes. Dana promptly accepted her offer. This was cool for Kayla, since her and Dana were single while Brandy was spending more time with her man.

It wasn't too long before Kayla ended her shift when Jeremy called. Just seeing his number on her cell phone made her cringe. She decided not to answer since she seriously didn't feel like dealing with him. Just as she pulled around the corner to her apartment, Jeremy was already sitting in the parking lot. She got out of the car, extremely pissed by his assertiveness. He had a lot of nerve to show up at her home without officially being invited. Why was he harassing her when he had a pregnant girlfriend he needed to attend to? He slowly got out of his car carrying a huge bouquet of red roses in his right hand.

"Hey, beautiful, you have a hard day at work today?"

"Jeremy, I thought I asked you to call me?"

"I did, but you didn't answer."

"I meant before showing up."

"What? Are you unhappy to see me or something, sweetie?"

Kayla just took a deep breath and headed towards the door of her downstairs apartment. Jeremy followed closely behind without saying another word. She opened the door and turned on the chandelier style light in the living room. He then walked ahead of her and voluntarily gave himself a tour.

"Nice place Hi-C," he said, trying to be funny.

"Yeah, thanks." His so–called humor didn't appease her at all.

"Some beautiful roses for the beautiful lady," he said as he handed them to her and sat down on the couch.

"Oh, how sweet, thanks." She was trying not to sound too repugnant, but she really hated his guts.

"You can go ahead and take your shower if you want to, I'll just watch a show or something and if you want me too, I can come in and wash your back like I use to."

She was trying to decide was he joking or had he seriously lost it. Even if she had manure on herself, she would have sat there in it until he left.

"Jeremy, I'm tired as hell so if there is anything that you feel you want to say, feel free to get it off your chest because I'll be going to bed soon."

"Well, you know about what I told you earlier right?" he began.

Kayla nodded her head in agreement as he continued. "You also know that I've wanted a kid for a while and how I feel about having kids and getting married. The problem is, she's having my baby but…I'm in love with you, so what type of solution can I come up with?"

"Therapy?" She couldn't believe she said that aloud.

"Actually, I was thinking of marrying you and later on convincing her to give us custody." He slowly eased a small box out of his pocket, got down on one knee and asked, "Will you marry me?"

It was right there when Kayla really knew that his mind was gone. She guessed the news of that woman being pregnant and whatever he was going through with his father had caused his normal logic to malfunction.

"For some reason, in your brain you've volunteered me to be a step-mom after you've cheated? Are you nuts?"

At that moment, she realized that he was serious. He had really conjured up a mastermind plan to live happily-ever-after with her and his unborn child. She could see the disappointment and anger in his eyes as he rose from the floor and got directly in her face as if he was purposely trying to intimidate her.

"What else do you think you are going to do, get some thug guy who won't do anything for you and cheat on you? All men cheat, Kayla, at least I take care of home."

"No, I'm going to get a man who isn't going to make me feel like I'm less then him and who doesn't disrespect me by calling me inhumane names."

"Grow up, Kayla, and quit crying. That's your problem now, you too proud with your stuck-up ass."

"But you are sitting here trying to marry me, huh?"

"Girl, please, women come a dime a dozen, I can do better than you."

"Good because that puts this ass back on the market."

It was at that point when he realized she no longer belonged to him. She had gotten her own apartment; she was paying her own bills, and didn't need him for anything. Not even the lousy lunch he tried to take her to earlier.

He suddenly grabbed her by her arms and pulled her in towards his body. He forced kisses on her neck while repeating how sorry he was. The more and more she struggled to pull away, the tighter his grip had gotten.

She was beyond terrified and had never been so helpless in her life. It felt as if some hobo had broken into her home and tried to attack her.

"GET OFF OF ME!" she screamed, hoping the next-door neighbors would hear her.

"I'd kill you if I ever even think you've been with somebody else," he raged as he pushed her against the wall.

She continued to scream but it didn't work. She made a swift move and butted him in the face with her forehead as hard as she could. He let go of his grasp and immediately checked his nose. She attempted to run towards the door as quickly as she could while trying to grab her cell phone from her back pocket. As soon as she got her hand on the doorknob, she felt his forceful hands grab her arm as he pulled her back to where he stood and backhand slapped her to the ground. He grabbed the cell phone and threw it up against the wall, breaking it into pieces. He then dragged her by the arms down the hall towards the bedroom while she attempted to kick wildly, frequently throwing him off his balance. He finally managed to get her in the room and then threw her on the bed and sat on her legs while holding her arms to the side.

"Do you realize how much time and money I put into you? For some reason you think another dude is about to reap the benefits. You're mine forever," he vented as he moved closer up on her torso, pinning her arms down with his knees. He began to pull off his shirt. She couldn't even cry. She was in so much shock and disbelief about what was happening in her very own home. He probably had been planning this entire episode since he found out she had an apartment. She just prayed someone would wake her up from this nightmare. What did she do to deserve such torment? How could a man she has known so long be on top of her about to rape her?

Partially Broken Never Destroyed II: Mirror Mirror

"Kayla, you will never believe what happened," assistant nurse, Rebecca, said as Kayla followed her to a private area. "Destiny is here in the hospital in critical condition."

"What!" Kayla gasped.

"Girl, yes! You know that everyone around here knew she was messing with a married man, so somehow, the wife found out, but that's not the sick part. Supposedly, the wife and the husband ended up tying her up, raping her, and then beating her."

"You're lying!" Kayla exclaimed.

"She is in section B1 of the intensive care unit. You can go see for yourself, and oh, don't tell anyone that I told you," Rebecca said, walking off.

Kayla didn't move. She was trying to process the information in her head. Rebecca had to have been exaggerating, she was known for doing that. Then again, maybe Rebecca was seeing how Kayla would react to the news knowing that Destiny was the one who had gotten her transferred.

Kayla wondered was Rebecca trying to see if she was involved. However, Rebecca couldn't stand Destiny either, since Destiny had slept with her ex-boyfriend, so she knew Rebecca hadn't reformed. She decided to go down to the ICU and see for herself.

<u>Chapter One</u>

"Donna, this wedding reception is nothing short of amazing!" Kelly bragged, one of Donna's coworkers.

"Thank you, girl. You learn to appreciate the finer things in life when your man wants nothing but the best for you. I told you two that this would be a day for everyone to remember."

"Yeah, I must say it's hard to top three fountains of Moët and Gucci watches for the entire wedding party. Now, you just got to make sure he's able to perform since he's almost twenty years your senior," Anthony stated.

"Don't mind him...I mean her," Kelly said as she nudged Anthony in the side.

"Oh, you know I'm not. Anthony probably just wants to get laid by my man because he's run out of men to lay at the office."

"You're lucky it's your wedding day and you look too beautiful for me to roast, bitch."

Beautiful was an understatement for the new Mrs. Donna Carter. Her backless dress accentuated her curvaceous hips as the inseams of her white, sequenced gown pulled closely together to showcase her supple breast. Even Beyoncé herself would have been wowed.

"Excuse me...uh...Kelly, if you don't mind I have to steal my wife for a moment." Troy interrupted, gently waltzing his new bride away from them.

"Did he really just act like I wasn't standing here? See, that's why I don't like his ass."

"I'm sure his ass is the only thing you do like," Kelly said as she snickered.

"No, I am not being funny. He is a total homophobic and that's not cool. Before you know it, he'll make her stop hangin' with us. Yes, you too, bitch, while you're looking all sideways at me."

"Did you forget that we all work at the same place?"

"Duh, he'll make her stop working, genius."

"Donna is not that weak-minded to quit her job."

"With all the money he got he can buy her a new job just like he bought his hair plugs."

"Something is seriously wrong with you," Kelly laughed. "Besides, even if she did quit, she wouldn't quit us."

"Well, either way someone needs to teach him a lesson in manners and acceptance."

"Calm down, Anthony. Don't get your panties in a bunch from over thinking. It could have been a simple oversight. He probably just didn't remember you."

"Bitch, no one forgets the queen. And for your info, I'm not wearing any panties."

"You are so nasty."

"Bitch, you don't know the half of it. Now, let's go get some drinks furbished by Mr. Anti-Homely himself."

Donna followed her husband, noticing that he had a tight squeeze on her hand. Observing that he didn't even acknowledge Anthony, this was probably going to be a brief spill about him being there. Donna didn't care. She knew her friends before she even met Troy, so she refused to let him dictate her relationships.

"What is that thing doing here?" Troy asked as they mingled on the dance floor.

"That is very disrespectful. Anthony is my friend," Donna stated, slightly agitated.

"Whatever it is; I told you that I didn't want it at my wedding."

"This isn't the wedding, it's the reception, and since when did you think that you were going to be able to choose my friends?"

"Thy shall not be disobedient to thine husband."

"Exactly. You are my husband, not my father."

"Perhaps someone should have been your father and taught you right from wrong."

"Are you really doing this on our wedding night?"

"Look, I have a business meeting in about an hour and a half. Finish up with your little friends, so we can still make our flight and I can spoil you in the Caribbean." He said, kissing her on the forehead and walking off to greet his daughter who was waving from the other side of the room to get his attention.

Donna hated when Troy would try to start an argument and then throw something extravagant in her face so that she wouldn't press the issue. Donna had expressed to Troy early on in the relationship that her mother and father both died in a car accident when she was seven. She went from foster home to foster home and the journey was beyond horrifying.

Although Troy sometimes had the jerkiest attitude about things, he treated her like a princess. Money wasn't an object since he was the carpeting tycoon of south Arizona. Besides, she was head-over-hills in love with Troy and would do just about anything to please him.

Troy was older and wasn't as physically active as Donna, but his magic stick still did the trick most of the time. The only drawback was that he couldn't last long unless he took Viagra, which ultimately gave him bad migraines.

Donna sometimes found herself pretending during sex, but Troy was the master at giving oral, which compensated for his stamina shortage. For a middle-aged man he was still very handsome and adventurous. He was actually about a ninety percent upgrade from all the other losers she had dated, so his minor flaws were acceptable.

The only other problem that Donna had was that she didn't like how Troy allowed his daughter to treat her. The nerve of her, Donna thought. Who allows their child to not only be absent from the wedding, but to show up at the reception and not speak? Now that Donna was officially moving into Troy's mansion, Monica had no choice but to abide by her rules whenever she came over to visit. She may not ever acknowledge her as her stepmother, but she sure in the hell was going to respect her as one.

"Monica, I'm glad you decided to come. I see you've changed your mind about your stepmother." Troy said, walking over to embrace his daughter Monica.

"Dad, she's not my mother. She's only about six or seven years older than me. Did you tell mom about the marriage?"

"Age is not defined with love, yet love is graced by infinite passion in youth," he said, totally ignoring her question.

"Yeah...sure, dad. I find it very convenient for a young office assistant to marry a rich mogul who technically could be her dad."

"Outside of love, the benefit of a union should go both ways. You would know that if you didn't have that son-of-a-bitch boyfriend leeching off of you."

"Dad, Eric is trying to open up his own fitness center. How is that leeching?"

"When was the last time he bought you something or paid for a date?"

"Dad, this isn't the time to discuss this. Listen, I need you to wire a thousand dollars in my account."

"Have you spoken to Donna yet?" He asked, totally ignoring her request.

"I was gonna-"

"So you have the guts to ask me for money on my wedding day, but you haven't even spoken to my wife?"

"I'm going now, dad. Could you wire the money now? Please and thank you." She added, walking over towards Donna.

"Hi, Donna. I came to say congratulations and you look nice." Monica stated, in the driest tone.

"Oh, is this your way of trying to act decent or did someone offer you some kind of incentive to talk to me."

"You know...whatever, Donna. You think you know everything, but you're no smarter than I am. We could have practically been in the same school together at some point."

"And it just burns you up that I'm the new apple of your daddy's eyes, doesn't it?

"Be careful what you say to me, Donna. You should always remember that I'll always be his daughter."

"That may be true, but now that we're married, I will always have access to the finances. I suggest you play nice. You wouldn't want the rent on your apartment to accidentally get defaulted."

As Monica walked off with a mean glare on her face, Donna knew that dealing with her was going to be challenging. She was the youngest daughter of her husband's two girls, so he had spoiled her rotten. Perhaps, Troy's missing ex-wife played a role in Monica's lack of respect for her.

Donna found it quite strange that she up and left the kids after the divorce. Although they were grown, it would seem as if she would at least stay in contact with her kids. Almost a year had passed and they heard nothing from her.

According to Troy, their mother did send them gifts with no return address for their birthdays and Christmas. Troy claimed that he loaned their mom some money before she left because she wanted to explore the world with her new friend guy. He also told the girls that their mom still randomly calls him from a private number to check on them. Donna just figured that she had a mental breakdown after the divorce and needed time to find herself. As selfish as it was, their mother being gone was one less person she had to deal with when it came to Troy.

"Drive!" Monica demanded to her boyfriend Eric, who was sitting in the car.

"What's your problem?"

"I literally hate that bitch!"

"Babe, that's his wife. You two are gonna have to find a way to get along."

"Not if I can help it."

"Babe, what are you plotting in that big, pretty head of yours?"

"Don't worry about it, Eric Bernard Ferguson."

"Hey! What did I tell you about calling me by my full name," he quickly said, playfully poking her in the neck.

"Stop!" She complained. "You're so annoying."

"And you're too damn sensitive. You need to just stay out of your dad's and Donna's business."

"Shut up and drive. I'm almost tempted to get rid of you just like I'm going to get rid of dirty Donna."

We Were Still Kids (Sample)

Charlie and Joey stood stiff as they looked at Jodie in awe. Joey was young enough to go for it, but Charlie was skeptical. She couldn't believe that Jodie was falling for it, too.

"He's a liar. How would he know our parents?" Charlie asked.

"Well, he asked me who did we stay with, and when I told him Grandma Rose, he said 'yeah, I know your parents. Y'all are those Johnson kids' and I hadn't told him anything," Jodie explained.

"Well, duh, that's my teacher, so I'm sure it wouldn't be hard for him to remember my last name," Charlie said in a matter-of-fact tone.

"Everybody knows he's just a temporary replacement for Ms. Kindle," teased Jodie.

"So?"

"So…what makes you think you're so special that he learned your last name in one day?"

"At least I don't believe everything I hear. You're more gullible than Joey and he's the youngest."

"And you're just mad he told me about mom and not you because he thinks I'm the pretty one," Jodie snapped back.

"Yeah, pretty ugly," Joey said, playfully pushing Jodie's arm and running towards the porch.

As Jodie ran after him towards the house, Charlie's feelings were hurt. Not because of what Jodie said about their looks; Charlie already knew Jodie was prettier than her. Charlie just didn't think that Mr. Frye would like Jodie more than he liked her.

About an hour or so later grandma had arrived home from work. Charlie was sitting in the front room sulking. She tried to hide her feelings, but she clearly wasn't good at it.

"Pick your face up, girl, before somebody step on it," said Grandma Rose as she walked toward the kitchen.

"Yes, grandma," she softly replied.

"What's the matter with you, Charlie?"

Charlie knew she couldn't hide anything from her grandma, but she didn't want to tell her what was bothering her. Charlie figured she'd whip her butt if she told her grandmother she was sad over something silly such as not being favored by a teacher.

"Everything was going fine until I got to homeroom this morning. We got a new teacher, grandma, and I'm not sure if things will work out," she finally said.

"Oh, it'll be okay, Charlie, I'm sure your teacher will like you just as much as the old teacher did. Now, go wash up for dinner."

"Ok, grandma."

Later that evening, Charlie quietly sat down at the dinner table and kept her mouth full, so she didn't have to do a lot of talking. Grandma told the others Charlie was upset because her old teacher was gone, but Jodie knew better. She knew she had crossed the line. Charlie could tell Jodie felt bad from the way she put her head down every time Charlie looked across the table at her.

After dinner, grandma made them clean up and get ready for bed. Joey had to get his hair brushed every night, so his eczema wouldn't flare up on his scalp. This gave Jodie a little time to talk to Charlie alone. She gave Charlie a push as they hopped in the bed.

"Are u still mad at me?" Jodie asked.

"No, who could stay mad at the prettiest girl in the world."

"Come on, really, Charlie? I didn't mean anything by it, besides; you are my sister, so you look just like me."

"I'm flattered," Charlie said, forging a fake smile.

"Come on, are we cool again, or do I have to call u a pretty toad for the rest of the week?"

They both started to laugh. They laughed so hard that grandma yelled to the back, giving them a warning as they scrambled to get in the bed. Feeling better, Charlie lay down and began to daydream about things she wanted to do on summer break.

"I love you, Charlie poop," Jodie said.

"I love you, too, beautiful toad," responded Charlie with a soft giggle and then they were both fast asleep.

It was finally Friday and the kids were happy that the weekend was approaching. Charlie wasn't as enthusiastic about her new teacher as she was the day before. She couldn't help but think he liked Jodie more than he did her. Jodie wasn't smarter than her or as funny as her. Jodie was only prettier than her and not by much. Charlie knew that teachers had their favorites, but good Lord; Jodie wasn't even in Mr. Frye's class. Maybe he just told Jodie about mom because she was older and assumed Jodie would better understand whatever he told her. On the other hand, Charlie knew it didn't matter because whatever he told Jodie about mom, Jodie would tell her.

Once school was over, Charlie went to meet up with Jodie and Joey outside by the school gymnasium. By the time she rounded the corner, she saw one of Joey's teachers standing with them with a big brown bag in her hand.

"Hey Charlie!" Jodie said as she ran up to her. "Guess what?"

"What?"

"Joey won the brown bag special in his class today!"

"What's the brown bag special?"

"It's fresh tomatoes, bell peppers, onions, carrots, and potatoes from Ms. Noel's garden."

Ms. Noel was the fourth-grade science teacher who had a green thumb. She would sporadically bring vegetables and fruits to school and one lucky kid in her class would win the collection in a drawing. Science was the only class Joey liked, so it was no surprise when he won.

Almost as if he had heard his name, Mr. Frye walked around the corner swinging his keys around his finger. Charlie began to wonder was he following them around the school. Why did he just seem to pop up when they were all together? Mr. Frye's humorous persona soon began to turn into annoyance.

"Hey kids. I found out in the teachers' lounge that little Joey won the brown bag surprise. Congratulations, sport!" He said, rubbing Joey's head.

"Yeah, I'm normally always in trouble, but not this time," Joey gleamed.

"Well, I'll be more than happy to give you guys a lift," offered Mr. Frye.

"No, we're taking the bus," blurted Charlie.

"Charlie, that's not polite. Sure, Mr. Frye, just drop us off where you left us the other day."

"Will do, I just have to stop by my house first."

"Jodie, you know grandma ain't about to play with us being late."

"It's fine, Charlie, trust me."

"No, I'm riding the bus," Charlie argued, storming off from them.

"Charlie, wait." Jodie said, catching up with her. "What's the real problem?"

Charlie couldn't admit that she was upset that her teacher seemed to favor her. It wasn't fair that everyone seemed to like Jodie. Joey had his science teacher, and they all had Grandma. Why couldn't Charlie have one person to herself?

"He's just becoming a weirdo and I don't like it."

"Yeah, but don't you wanna know about momma?"

"Yeah, but-"

"Come on, Charlie poop, I got this. We'll be home before grandma even knows anything."

Charlie was skeptical as she allowed Jodie to grab her hand as she followed her older sister. There was an eerie feeling running through Charlie's veins that she just couldn't shake. It didn't take being a psychic for Charlie to sense something was about to go wrong.

The Doctor's Inn: A Private Practice (Sample)

Part II Now Available

"Brad!" she cried. "Stop it, please."

"Let me go!" He demanded.

"You can't do this! You love me!"

Brad flung open the door and shoved her out. He glared at her, his eyes starting to glaze over as tears fought to break out. "I loved you. But I was a fool. I am done being your play toy. Find another sucker to play your game. Goodbye, Jenna."

He stepped back, away from the threshold, and then he slammed the door, shutting out Jenna's lying face. If he could he would shut out his bitter reality. It was a solemn moment for him. If only he could rewind the instance and not had went for her phone at all.

The living room seemed to spin around him, and he felt himself free-falling. Seven years ago, he had thought he found a rose. How was he to know that the beautiful woman was nothing but a thorn in a roses clothing? She continued to slam her hand against the door as she begged him to talk to her. He stood there on the opposite side, almost tempted to open it but he couldn't. He couldn't allow her to make a mockery of him by trying to justify something that was evident.

She finally gave in by telling him she was going to go to her mom's house. She suggested that he needed some time to cool off and rationalize things. He peeked through the window and watched her slowly walk away while calling someone on her cell phone.

Clutching his head as though he would crack it open, he dropped listlessly on a couch. He still couldn't believe what had transpired in a matter of minutes. He then performed an act he had not attempted since his childhood. It was an act he thought he had outgrown. He wept.